To: Dorothy
Helen

DUCK HUNTING WITH GRANDPA

by Helen White Hunter

Illustrations by Grant Rozeboom

The Young American Hunting and Fishing Series©

Hunter House Publications

Duck Hunting With Grandpa
© Copyright 1998
Helen Hunter

Second Printing 2000.

Illustrations by Grant Rozeboom

Published by Hunter House Publications
1132 21st Street S.E.
Cedar Rapids, IA 52403

Printed in the United States of America

Library of Congress Cataloging-in-Publication Data

Hunter, Helen
    Duck Hunting With Grandpa / by Helen Hunter
    illustrations, Grant Rozeboom – 1st ed.
    p. cm (The Young American Hunting & Fishing Series; 1)
    Summary: A young boy learns duck hunting skills and techniques, and wildlife conservation. Warm relationships are built with grandfather and his friends in training hunting dogs, in the duck blind, and at the hunting cabin.
    ISBN 0-96627-690-6
    [1. Boys and Girls–Fiction. 2. Fathers–Fiction. 3. Grandfathers–Fiction. 4. Duck Hunting–Fiction.]

                                                        98-92611
                                                        CIP
                                                        AC

To Bud
for the memories and
relationships that have been built
and continue to grow
through the sport of
duck hunting.

Helen Hunter

In Loving Memory of
my grandfather,
Jack Hahn,
from whom I learned to draw
and who gave me a
love of wildlife and hunting.

Grant Rozeboom

TABLE OF CONTENTS

Chapter One   Grandpa's Early Hunts   1

Chapter Two   Gun Safety   9

Chapter Three   Equipment   21

Chapter Four   Duck Hunting Residences   35

Chapter Five   The Hunt   45

Chapter Six   Water and Boating Safety   63

Chapter Seven   Puddle Ducks   79

Chapter Eight   Cleaning the Ducks   88

A Hunter's Pledge   95

Endnotes   96

CHAPTER ONE

GRANDPA'S EARLY HUNTS

"How did you learn how to hunt?" I asked Grandpa one day.

"When I was a young lad your age I lived in Kansas City, Missouri," said Grandpa. "My dad was not a hunter and neither was my grandpa, so they couldn't teach me to hunt."

"Did you already have a gun?" I asked.

"Not until my uncle went to service with the United States Navy," Grandpa answered. "Then he gave me permission to use his gun while he was away. It was a .12–*gauge* Model 97 Winchester pump gun."

*   *Words in italics are explained at the end of each chapter.*

1

When Grandpa was a young boy he rode the city bus to go hunting for rabbits.

Grandpa's first hunting experience was not with ducks. He hadn't even thought of hunting ducks.

"I used to get on the bus with my gun and a *gunny sack* and go to the end of the bus line. The end of the line was way out on the edge of the city. Almost like being in the country," said Grandpa. "But that was way back in the early 1940s."

I laughed when I thought about getting on a bus with a gun.

"Kids wouldn't be able to do that today." I said. "They'd get in big trouble—even if the gun was in a case."

"Don't ever do it," Grandpa agreed. He added, "Do you know what I hunted out there at the end of the bus line?"

"Rabbits?" I guessed.

"You're right! How did you know?"

"I'm your Grandson, that's how," I replied, teasing Grandpa like he teases me.

Grandpa told how he tramped through the brushy fields shooting rabbits until he got his limit.

"I don't recall how many rabbits you could take. I either got my limit, or I ran out of shotgun shells. Whichever came first."

3

"I skinned the rabbits I shot and put them in the gunny sack," Grandpa said. "Then I waited for the bus and took my *game* home for my mother to cook."

Because he enjoyed hunting so much, and brought so much wild game home, his mother persuaded him to find other people who could use the extra rabbits.

"One day after I got home a neighbor came up to me," Grandpa said. "He said if I'd give him the rabbits before I skinned them, he would trade them for shotgun shells."

Grandpa never had to buy another box of shells after meeting old Mr. Larson. Not until he was older, that is.

"Hunting for rabbits was great practice for the hunting I would do when I was older," Grandpa said. "But enough about my escapades. It's time for you to learn how to hunt, too."

"When did you start hunting ducks?" I asked. I loved to hear Grandpa tell all his old stories.

"When I was in college at the University of Iowa, two of my friends and I bought hunting licenses," Grandpa said. He got that faraway look in his eyes while he thought about who those friends were and where they went to hunt.

"We didn't have a boat. We didn't even have any hunting gear—no waders or

camouflage clothing," Grandpa said with a laugh. "But we took our guns and went to a creek out in the country. We walked along the shore and tried to scare up some ducks. One of us had a *duck call*."

"Did you get some ducks?"

"I shot my first duck that day. A wood duck," Grandpa said. "We sure had a good time."

Grandpa has been teaching me what I need to learn so that I can be a good hunter and a good *conserva-tionist*. I hope you'll enjoy what I have learned from my grandfather.

HUNTING VOCABULARY

CAMOUFLAGE – the use of paint, leaves, and patterns which blend with nature's colors and back-ground; used to hide or conceal.

CONSERVATIONIST – a person who believes in protecting, conserving and managing the earth's natural resources and wildlife.

DUCK CALL – a wooden or plastic instrument used to imitate the sound of a duck.

GAME – wild birds or animals hunted for sport or for use as food.

GAUGE – a unit of measurement. For example, twelve round lead balls the same diameter as the interior of the gun's barrel will weigh one pound.

GUNNY SACK – a sack or bag made of hemp, a coarse, heavy fabric which is also used to make rope and sailcloth.

7

CHAPTER TWO

GUN SAFETY

It took time to learn gun safety. Grandpa started teaching me how to handle guns safely when I was about five years old. My first 'gun' was carved out of wood. It wasn't a gun at all. It was just wood shaped like a gun.

When I was seven years old, he gave me a *BB gun*. BB pellets are the smallest and weakest *ammunition*. There is no gunpowder in them at all. They are pushed out of the gun with *compressed air*. Still, if you get hit with them, at the very least they sting.

"Some people have been injured by BBs. They can put out an eye very quickly," Grandpa said, "so you have to be very careful just the same as with a grown up's gun."

9

Grandpa taught me that if someone is walking in front of me, I should put my gun over my shoulder so the *muzzle* is pointing behind me, or across my chest with the muzzle pointed toward the sky.

"But what if you're walking in front?" asked Grandpa. "How would you carry your gun?"

"With the muzzle pointing at the ground," I answered.

"Right!" said Grandpa.

When climbing over a fence, I learned to hand the gun to Grandpa. Then I held both his gun and mine while he climbed over. When we sat down to rest, we laid our guns on the ground with the *shells or cartridges* out of the *chambers*, and pointed away from us. If the gun had a *safety* it was in the 'on' position.

"The same thing is true about leaning our guns against a tree," Grandpa said. "If it wasn't unloaded and it happened to tip over, the gun might fire."

We did target practice with our BB guns, shooting at tin cans which we set up on fence posts or tree stumps in a friend's field.

"Always be sure you ask for permission to be there," Grandpa said, "and make sure there are no farm animals or people around."

We shot at tin cans for target practice.

We made sure there was a tall bank behind the stumps so it stopped the BBs.

Learning to sight down the barrel of the gun was a real trick. The first few times I shot my BB gun, I didn't hit a single thing. But I kept trying—aiming, squinting one eye and sighting with the other, making sure I could see that the tin can was in the notch on the gun's barrel. Finally I was able to hit the target almost every time.

"Shooting a shotgun at moving ducks will be more difficult than shooting tin cans with a BB gun," Grandpa said.

"Because they're moving targets, right?" I guessed.

"Yes, you'll have to learn to *compensate* for different angles, ranges, and flight speeds. And all of that has to be done within seconds," Grandpa said. "After you get the hang of shooting at targets that don't move, we'll give a try at shooting at *clay pigeons*."

"What do you shoot clay pigeons with, Grandpa?"

"Well, first of all you use a shotgun." Grandpa grinned. "How do you like your clay pigeons cooked?"

"Grandpa! Quit teasing," I said, grinning back. "I know you use a shotgun. I meant what kind of ammunition?"

Grandpa explained that you can buy three kinds of *loads*: light loads, medium loads, and magnum, or heavy, loads.

"You can use the lightest or least expensive shells for shooting clay pigeons, which is also called *trap shooting*," Grandpa explained.

"Are they different from what you use when you're really shooting ducks?" I asked. "What kind of shell do you use then?"

"Most duck hunters like heavier loads," Grandpa explained. "And they can't use lead shot when hunting *migratory* water fowl."

Boy, I thought, hunting is complicated. There are lots of things you have to know.

"Currently, steel shot is the most popular for waterfowl," said Grandpa, "although there are several other approved types available."

"Like what?"

"Oh, the names of them are *tungsten* and *bismuth*," Grandpa said, "but there aren't many of these types manufactured right now and they cost more than twice as much as steel shot."

13

On another day Grandpa showed me how the safety features of a shotgun are the same as those I had learned with a BB gun. In addition, he cautioned me about making sure the safety was on when I had a shell in the chamber.

I had already learned the importance of where the gun was pointing and was careful not to pass the barrel of the gun by someone's head or body.

"Guns demand respect," Grandpa said. "One of the ten commandments of firearm safety is never point a gun at anything you do not want to shoot. Another one is that every gun is to be treated with the respect due a loaded weapon."

I wanted to be very careful. I didn't want to shoot Grandpa, a friend, or one of our dogs.

"You have manners at the dinner table," Grandpa said. "That's because you have learned to have consideration for others. Gun safety is even more important. If you have manners, you'll always think of how your behavior will affect others."

Grandpa says that a good place for boys and girls to learn about gun safety and how to shoot is at a fire arms safety class or a hunter education program.

"Every state sponsors some type of class," Grandpa

14

said. "Many states require beginning hunters to pass such a course before they can purchase a license.

"If you ever hunt without me," said Grandpa, "and your friends break any of these rules, don't hunt with them! It's too dangerous."

When I turned eleven years old, Grandpa gave me a 20-gauge shotgun for my birthday.

The 20-gauge was still a little bit heavy for me, but it wouldn't be long until I managed it well.

"There is one smaller shotgun which you could have had—a .410," Grandpa said. "But they are harder to shoot because they are so small. The .410 is the only shotgun measured in inches rather than balls per pound," Grandpa explained. "It is .41 one hundredths of an inch inside the barrel."

I didn't really understand the difference, but Grandpa said someday I would.

"Besides," Grandpa continued, "we can use only *steel shot* to hunt ducks and the factories make only steel shot in shells for 10-gauge, 12-gauge, and 20-gauge guns."

TEN COMMANDMENTS OF FIREARM SAFETY

1. Treat every gun with the respect due a loaded weapon.

2. Watch that muzzle! Be able to control the direction of the muzzle even if you should stumble. Keep the *safety* on until you are ready to shoot.

3. Be sure the barrel and action are clear of *obstructions* and that you have the proper size of *ammunition* for the gun you are carrying.

4. Always unload your gun when not in use. Open the *actions* or *take the gun down*. Guns should be carried in cases to the shooting area.

5. Be sure of your target before you pull the trigger. Know identifying features of the wildfowl or game you hunt.

6. Never point a gun at anything you do not want to shoot. Avoid all *horseplay* with a firearm.

7. Never climb a fence or tree or jump a ditch with a loaded gun. Never pull a gun toward you by the muzzle.

8. Never shoot a bullet at a flat, hard surface, or water because bullets can *ricochet*, or bounce back at you. At target practice be sure your backstop is adequate.

9. Store guns and ammunition separately and beyond the reach of small children and careless adults.

10. Avoid alcoholic beverages before or during shooting.

HUNTING VOCABULARY

ACTIONS – the moving parts, or mechanisms of the gun.

AMMUNITION – bullets, gunpowder, shot, shells.

BB GUN – sometimes called an air rifle because it uses compressed air to shoot the BBs. A BB is a single .18 inch–in–diameter solid ball, a little larger than a No. 2 pencil lead.

BISMUTH – a hard, brittle, metallic chemical element used to make ammunition.

CHAMBER – the part of the gun that holds the shell or cartridge.

CLAY PIGEONS – shaped like a small frisbee, brittle saucer–like disks of baked clay which are tossed into the air from a trap to be shot at as a target.

COMPENSATE – to make allowances for a variation.

COMPRESSED AIR – air reduced in volume and held in a small container.

HORSEPLAY – rough and noisy fun.

LEAD SHOT – a heavy metal formed into small balls.

LOAD – a single charge, as of powder and bullets, for a firearm.

MIGRATORY – wildfowl, animals and fish that move from one place to another because of the change of seasons.

MUZZLE – the front end of the barrel of a firearm.

OBSTRUCTIONS – anything that blocks or stops the action or barrel of a gun.

RICOCHET – the rebound of a bullet or a stone which strikes a surface at an angle.

SAFETY – the catch or locking device on a firearm which keeps it from firing.

SHELL OR CARTRIDGE – the metal or plastic case which contains the charge, or the load, and the primer, a small cap or tube which holds the explosive.

STEEL SHOT – is required for duck hunting rather than shot made of lead. Ducks scoop lead up from the bottom of the lake or pond thinking it is something to eat. After digestion the lead kills them.

TAKE THE GUN DOWN – taking the gun apart.

TRAP SHOOTING – a machine throws disks, called clay pigeons, into the air for shooting.

TUNGSTEN – a hard, heavy, gray–white, metallic chemical element used to make shot.

CHAPTER THREE

EQUIPMENT

THE HUNTING DOG

"I've had several good hunting dogs over all the years I've hunted," Grandpa said. "Some of them were better than others. I spent a lot of money training a couple of my Labs. One of them never did learn, and I had to give him away for a pet."

Grandpa said that a poorly trained dog is worse than no dog at all. If your dog won't obey you, you can't take him hunting with you.

"Every duck hunter needs a good water dog or *retriever*," Grandpa said. "We have a good one in Buck. He's a great hunting dog!"

Late in the summer—way before duck hunting

season—Grandpa liked to 'refresh Buck's memory' about how to retrieve.

We got three *dummies* out of the garage.

"Dogs handle the dummy just like they do a bird," Grandpa said, "carrying it gently in their mouths without digging their teeth into it."

Buck sat and watched when Grandpa threw out the first dummy. But he didn't chase it. He marked, or watched, where the dummy landed. At Grandpa's command he raced out to bring it in.

"Back," Grandpa said and he pointed with his arm. When Buck brought the dummy back, he delivered it to Grandpa's hand. He was trained to sit by Grandpa's left leg and wait for the next command. Buck loved to retrieve. When he was excited, he trembled.

"Buck, like all dogs, was trained with single word commands," Grandpa said. "My good friend, Errol Montgomery, trained Buck."

"Here, you can throw one, too."

Grandpa handed me a dummy. We each tossed one as far out on the lawn as we could, sending them in different directions. Buck sat. He waited for Grandpa to give the retrieve command. Grandpa ran his hand along Buck's head toward one of the dummies.

Every duck hunter needs a good retriever.

23

"Back," Grandpa said.

Buck went after the dummy Grandpa had tossed. He brought it back quickly. When Grandpa said 'back' again, he hurried to bring in the one I threw. We worked Buck for about fifteen minutes. We threw as many as three dummies at the same time. He brought each one back and awaited the next command.

Before Buck got tired, we put him back in his kennel for a drink and a rest.

Grandpa said every retriever has his own hunting behavior, perking his ears or wagging his tail rapidly.

"When we go hunting with Buck, you will see Buck's hunting personality," Grandpa said. "He behaves differently when there are real ducks."

"Have you always had a black Labrador?" I asked.

"My best old hunting buddy was a yellow Lab. His name was Sarge," Grandpa said. "He's been gone for a long time."

Grandpa was a little bit sad about not having Sarge anymore. I could tell when he talked about him.

"But I've also hunted with a Chesapeake Retriever, too. He was also a good duck hunter," Grandpa added. "But there are other kinds of retrievers that work well for duck hunting—like golden retrievers and American water spaniels."

"Why are those kinds of dogs so good for duck hunting? Are they smarter?"

"Yes, they're smart. And all of them are bred to be hunters. But the Labrador's, the Chesapeake's and the American water spaniel's skin secretes oil," Grandpa said. "That helps their coats shed the water. Then they don't get so cold in fall's icy water."

Grandpa said they are all excellent swimmers, too.

"Some people think that a Lab's feet are webbed for swimming," Grandpa said.

HUNTING GEAR

You could hunt for ducks like my grandfather did when he was in college, but you probably wouldn't be the most successful duck hunter around. He didn't have any hunting gear or camouflage clothing. He could hunt only from the bank of the stream.

To be successful, duck hunters need to have some hunting gear. I'm glad my grandfather has gear for me. I wouldn't be able to buy it from my allowance. But when I get older, I'll buy things for myself.

Decoys

"Besides a shotgun and a good dog duck hunters need to have a good supply of *decoys.*" Grandpa said, "Decoys come in lots of different materials, like cork, wood, pressed paper, foam, and hollow plastic."

"I remember that battery operated tipping duck decoy that you got for Christmas a couple of years ago?" I said. I remembered because it was so funny looking. It had no head and no body, only tail feathers of the duck sticking up in the air.

"That's what mallard ducks look like when they're feeding," Grandpa said. "They dip their heads and part of their backs in the water. Their tail feathers and feet are all that show, and they wiggle in the water."

"Could you still use those old decoys in your basement?" I wondered.

"Some hunters still use old wooden decoys, but many of them, like those in my basement, have become valuable collector's items," Grandpa said.

"Decoys can look like different duck species, too. There are canvasbacks, mallards, wood ducks and half a dozen other kinds."

When Grandpa and his friends hunt, they use decoys that look like mallards—both *drakes* and *hens*—because that is the kind of duck they hunt. Their purpose is to make flying ducks think that other ducks are already sitting on the lake or pond.

Grandpa got a decoy from the garage.

"See this long cord? And the weight hanging at the end of it?" Grandpa showed me what he was talking about. "The depth of the water determines how much cord is used and how far the weight is dropped to rest on the lake bottom. It operates like an anchor. It keeps the decoy from floating away, but the amount of string allows the decoy to move in the water."

Camouflage Clothing

"A water-*repellent,* warm hunting jacket is essential for duck hunting," Grandpa said, "and a hat with ear flaps."

Grandpa said that having enough clothes to stay warm is most important. Gloves and waders—either hip or chest—are also good duck hunting gear.

Everything my grandpa uses is camouflage colored—even his long john underwear! He has camouflage seat cushions and a backpack. He has a camouflage painted box to keep his cooking utensils in. He even covered his thermos bottle with camouflage tape.

"The reason you use camouflage clothing for duck hunting," Grandpa said, "is because the colors of the clothing all blend into the ducks' *habitat*."

"If you wore a bright orange vest or hat, like you do for deer hunting, the ducks might see you from miles away, and they might not come to your call," Grandpa said. "Especially if you were moving," he added. "You'll notice that when we are in the woods or on the lake **our** eyes go right away to anything that moves. It's the same for the ducks."

I learned that not moving when the ducks are nearby is even more important than the camouflage clothing.

"You can wear any dark color to blend in with your background," Grandpa said, "but sit or stand still. If you can, get in the shadows and keep the sun from reflecting off your face or glasses."

Binoculars

With Grandpa's binoculars, you can see ducks clearly from a long distance away. I like to use a small pair of Grandpa's that are also camouflaged.

"Looking through the binoculars helps us determine what kind of birds are flying," Grandpa said. "They might be ducks. But they also might be crows or *cormorants*. Or it might be a flock of *Canada geese*."

Grandpa told a story about how his sons and their friends used to play tricks with the binoculars during times when there weren't many ducks flying.

"One of the boys fell asleep once," Grandpa said with a chuckle. "The others rubbed soot from the fire around the edges of the binoculars. When the guy woke up and used the binoculars the next time, he had black circles around his eyes for the rest of the day. Oh, how they all laughed at him."

Duck Calls

Several years ago Grandpa and Mr. Montgomery decided to make duck calls and sell them.

"How did you know how to make duck calls?"

"We **didn't** know how," Grandpa said. "We had to learn. We drove to several wood mills in the area and bought pieces of wood—cherry, walnut, *hedge apple*, and several other kinds. Then we made patterns on the *lathe* in my workshop."

Grandpa said it took a long time to get the pattern just right.

"Then we went to work turning the barrels of the calls, sanding and polishing them until they shone. We even put shiny metal bands around some of them."

That was the easy part.

"Making the 'insides' for the call was much more difficult," Grandpa said.

"What goes on the inside?" I asked.

"That's the part that holds the *reed* which makes the call squawk and sound like a duck. It is kind of like the reed that's in a clarinet or a saxophone."

Grandpa and Mr. Montgomery both decided after a short time of production that the duck call manufacturing business wasn't for them. They stopped making them and started buying their new duck calls from the local sporting goods store.

"The cost of a duck call is only a small factor in finding a good call," Grandpa said. "Some of the best

30

ones are the lowest priced. And some of the most expensive are not as good."

"Does it take a long time to learn?" I asked.

"Blowing a duck call takes lots of practice," Grandpa said. "Some people listen to tapes to learn how to call. 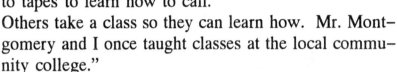 Others take a class so they can learn how. Mr. Montgomery and I once taught classes at the local community college."

"It's a good idea to ask someone who hunts ducks to suggest a duck call you can afford," Grandpa said. "But remember, you'll never learn to blow it if you keep it in your pocket."

"Remember when you gave me my first duck call, Grandpa? You said I was one year old."

"You were. It was one that I had made. You blew into it and it squawked, and I knew right then that you were going to be a duck hunter. If you get really good," Grandpa said, "there are duck calling contests you can enter and win prizes."

"You mean **when** I get good, don't you, Grandpa?" I teased. "Cause with you teaching me, I'll be good!"

"Contests are great fun," Grandpa said. "Local contest winners can compete for the Championship of the World in Stuttgart, Arkansas."

Folks come from all over the world to compete and to listen to the callers. When Grandpa competed there was a junior contest, a ladies contest, and the open contest.

"Then every five years the champions of the past five years compete for the 'Champion of Champions' contest."

One year my grandpa was the Iowa State Duck Calling Champion. After he won the Iowa contest, he got to compete in Stuttgart, Arkansas. He didn't win that contest, but a very good friend of his did.

HUNTING VOCABULARY

CANADA GEESE – is the correct name, though many people call them 'Canadian' geese.

CORMORANTS – from the family of large, black diving birds with webbed toes and a hooked beak.

DECOY – an artificial bird used to lure game to a place where it can be shot.

DRAKE – a male duck.

DUMMY – a canvas bag stuffed with *kapok*, or made out of plastic.

HABITAT – the place where a plant or animal naturally grows or lives.

HEDGE APPLE – a small thorny tree of the mulberry family. It has hard, yellow wood. Often used for hedges, it has greenish–yellow, inedible fruit.

HEN – a female duck.

KAPOK – the silky fibers around the seeds of several silk–cotton trees which is used for stuffing in mattresses, life preservers and sleeping bags, and dummies for training dogs.

LATHE – a machine used for shaping an article of wood.

REED – a strip of some flexible substance, as cane, metal, or plastic which vibrates when blown on and produces a sound.

REPELLENT – resists absorbing the water. Repellent does not mean it is water–proof.

RETRIEVER – a dog trained to find and bring back birds and some other small game.

CHAPTER FOUR

DUCK HUNTING RESIDENCES

THE DUCK BLIND

"Who thought of making a duck blind?" I asked.

"I don't know who thought of putting it on top of a boat," Grandpa said, "but people have been making blinds since they started hunting."

"What kind of blinds?"

"Your imagination is the limit—willows, tall weeds, driftwood on the shore, canvas, netting—anything to hide you from the ducks," Grandpa said.

Grandpa has his own duck blind. It's like a shed or shelter built over the top of his eighteen–foot *john boat*. The metal is painted with drab colors—greens and browns that blend in with the colors of fall.

"The blinds that we use today probably got their start in Iowa—right at Lake Odessa—around forty or fifty years ago.

"Late in the summer we'll touch up the paint to cover any faded places," Grandpa said. "Then we'll go gather some pin oak branches and *arborvitae*, a special type of evergreen."

I've helped Grandpa and his friends push the branches and the evergreens through the *wire* that covers the boat. When we're finished it looks like a timber on top of a boat.

On the back of the blind was an outboard motor and inside were batteries for the lights, a cook stove, and several propane heaters.

"See this nice place in front," Grandpa said. "It's a place for Buck. He can sit outside and watch what's going on while we hunt from inside."

The day we hooked the duck blind on the back of Grandpa's *Suburban* was an exciting day. Buck got into his portable kennel in the back of the truck. He was excited, too.

We always went 'down to the lake' the afternoon before the hunt.

36

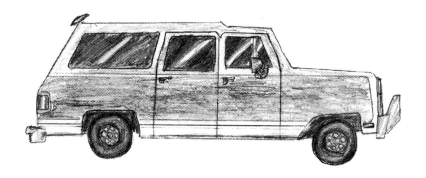

"If we didn't go the day before, what time would we have to leave in the morning so we would be at Lake Odessa in time to hunt?" I asked Grandpa.

"We'd have to get up in the middle of the night to make the drive and then *launch* the boat in the dark," Grandpa answered. "It's much better to get to the lake early, get the blind in the water, and have time to settle in while it is still light."

We hunted at Lake Odessa during the fall duck seasons. On the way to Lake Odessa, we stopped to pick up Mr. Montgomery.

"Can you guess how long Montgomery and I have hunted together?" Grandpa asked.

I didn't guess.

Grandpa said he and Montgomery have hunted together for thirty years. When we stopped at his place to pick him up, Grandpa and Montgomery shook hands and exchanged greetings. They loaded his gear into the Suburban.

"Hi, Mr. Montgomery," I said.

"Hi, kid. You can call me Montgomery. When you say 'Mister' it makes me feel old." He mussed my hair.

When we were on the road again Grandpa asked, "Do you know what the three parts of hunting are?"

I had heard this before.

"Let's see, one part is getting ready . . ."

"Yup, that's *anticipation*."

"Another part is hunting," I said, "but I can't remember the word for that."

"*Participation*," Grandpa said. "And then *recollection*. There is a certain ceremony in each part."

I watched the scenery and listened to Grandpa and Montgomery talking with each other. When we made the last turn on the road to the lake the excitement mounted—not only for Grandpa Hunter, Montgomery and me, but even for Buck, the dog.

Buck whined and became restless in his kennel. He seemed to know he was an important part of duck season.

As we pulled into the clearing we could see the lake. Part of Lake Odessa is a wildlife refuge where ducks can rest without being hunted. The other part is open for hunting.

Fall had arrived in Iowa for sure. Duck hunters who didn't have a dock had *staked out* places and pulled their duck blinds up on the sandy shore. The blinds were covered with *foliage* designed to fool the ducks. Every one of them was different.

"Whose blind is the best?" Grandpa asked.

"No contest!" I answered. "Ours!"

Grandpa let Montgomery out at the dock, then drove to the launching area and backed the duck blind into the water. I held on to the rope while he parked the Suburban. Then we both hopped in and motored around to the dock. Montgomery tied the duck blind up for the night.

After the boat was docked and safe for the night, we walked across the wide lawn and climbed the steps to Grandpa's Lake Odessa hunting cabin.

THE CABIN

Grandpa has told me stories about some of the cabins he has stayed in when he hunted—from Alaska to Mexico and points in between. One was in the mountains and woods along the Missouri and Arkansas border.

"I thanked Mr. Green for letting me use his hunting shack," Grandpa said. "Mr. Green said, 'That isn't a shack. It's my hunting cabin.' It was one room with a stone fireplace, an old couch, a small wood table, and two chairs.

"There were no beds, no electricity or running water," Grandpa explained. "The toilet was outdoors and very *primitive*."

Hearing those stories made Grandpa's cabin at Lake Odessa seem like a palace.

"I sure like our cabin," I told Grandpa.

"Grandma has almost ruined it," Grandpa said. "I used to bring her here when it was just an old wreck of a place. And look what she's done to it!" Grandpa swung his arm around the room to show me the terrible things Grandma had done.

I didn't see anything bad. I had been coming to Lake Odessa since I was a little boy. I had grown up with it just the way it was. With one look back at Grandpa's face, I knew he was teasing me. Again.

While Grandpa and Montgomery got settled, I looked at the familiar things that welcomed us to Lake Odessa—the black iron stove in the corner that crackled with a warm fire, the Canada goose hanging above the stove, her wings spread for landing. And even the things that Grandma has contributed—the stacks of books and games, the curtains and rugs.

The bulletin board behind the kitchen door fascinated me.

"Grandpa, tell me again about the dollar bills tacked on the bulletin board." Each dollar bill had a message written to Grandpa.

"It has been a *tradition* for each person who stays here at Lake Odessa to leave a *sentiment* about how much he enjoyed the hunt," Grandpa said. "One time someone tacked up a dollar bill. He wrote a note on it and after that, everyone who stayed here left a dollar."

Many men have hunted at Lake Odessa over the years and stayed in Hunter's cabin—quite a few when Grandpa wasn't even there. They wrote on the dollar bills things like, "Brrr. Cold hunt this morning. Got our limit." Or, "No ducks flying. Beautiful day." Or, "Thanks for the great resting place." Once a married couple stayed, and they left a **two** dollar bill with a note on it. I kind of like that one.

After eating our supper and playing a game of cards, Grandpa said, "It's time to hit the sack. Morning is going to come awfully quick."

I liked the top bunk, and none of Grandpa's friends quarreled with me about climbing up there. This time only Grandpa and I slept in the little square bedroom with the two sets of bunks. Montgomery liked to sleep on the couch. We heard him snoring through the closed bedroom door.

"He's been snoring like that for thirty years," Grandpa said with a chuckle. "Good thing we're sound sleepers."

HUNTING VOCABULARY

ANTICIPATION – to look forward to, like a pleasant vacation.

ARBORVITAE – a tree or shrub with evergreen–like leaves.

FOLIAGE – decorations consisting of leaves and branches from trees and plants.

JOHN BOAT – a flat–bottomed boat with square ends used on inland waters.

LAUNCH – to set the boat afloat.

PARTICIPATION – to share with others in some activity.

PRIMITIVE – crude, simple, or rough.

RECOLLECTION – a time of remembering an event.

SENTIMENT – feeling or opinion, often with emotion.

STAKED OUT – Tall metal stakes are pounded into the shore for the duck blinds to pull between to keep the boats from being blown sideways and getting the motors stuck in the sand.

SUBURBAN – a sports vehicle or truck made by Chevrolet or GMC.

TRADITION – a custom or practice observed by a group of people.

WIRE – a lightweight, pliable wire constructed into a fence, like what might be used for a garden or to keep chickens in a pen.

CHAPTER FIVE

THE HUNT

"I sure slept good," Montgomery said. "I'll bet I didn't make a peep in the night."

Grandpa and I just grinned at each other. Neither of us had slept much—not just because of Montgomery's snoring but because it was hard to go to sleep just thinking about hunting the next day.

It was still dark at three o'clock in the morning. Everyone was up and had taken a turn in the bathroom. Buck had slept on the front porch. His toenails clicked on the floor as he eagerly waited for us to let him out.

"Get yourself some camouflage clothing," Grandpa said.

Camouflage clothing of every size and shape— pants, shirts and jackets—hung on the back porch rack.

45

I chose a camouflage shirt. Even the smallest one worn over my winter jacket was too big. But I put it on anyway and rolled up the sleeves. The shirt hung down to my knees.

All of us were covered in olive drab and camouflage clothes. We sat down at the kitchen table to eat a bowl of cold cereal.

"This will tide us over until we have a 'real' breakfast later," Grandpa said.

Grandpa and Montgomery put their chest waders on and hiked the suspenders over their shoulders. Then they put on their warm hunting jackets and caps.

Everyone picked up something to carry down to the dock—the thermos bottles, the grocery bag of food, and the shotguns.

Stars twinkled in the early morning sky when Grandpa, Montgomery, and I got into the duck blind.

Grandpa whistled for Buck.

"Come, Buck," he called. Buck jumped on the front of the boat.

*The duck blinds were covered with foliage
designed to fool the ducks.*

The air was frosty cold. Our breath made white, puffy vapors in the October morning.

Several duck blinds were already motoring across the lake, making their way to favorite hunting spots.

We motored out to "The Breaks." That's the spot that Grandpa and Montgomery like best. There we would get 'set up'. On the way the wind was cold. We huddled inside the blind.

Getting set up meant putting the blind back in the reeds and bushes with the wind at our backs. When the duck blind was pushed back into the bank of the lake you almost couldn't see it. It looked like it was part of the timber.

There was room on the front of the boat for Buck to sit without being covered. Buck watched for ducks, too.

The next job was putting out the decoys.

"You'll have to grow quite a bit taller before you can do this," Grandpa said. "In some places the water is deeper than you are tall."

Grandpa took off his warm coat and hiked up his chest waders. He eased himself over the edge of the boat, taking an oar to steady himself in the water. Montgomery handed him duck decoys one at a time.

Grandpa threw them out into the lake. The line and the weight floated away from the decoy body and anchored them in the water. Grandpa liked to spread the decoys out because the kind of ducks we were hunting were puddle ducks, or shallow water ducks.

"The decoys make real ducks think other ducks are sitting on the pond," Grandpa explained. "When wild ducks spot the decoys, they often circle and land, thinking they have found a good place to eat and rest."

Grandpa got back into the boat. The water from his waders made puddles on the floor of the boat. He opened up the shooting hatches along the side of the boat. Then we saw the lake. When we leaned out a little bit, we could see the sky and watch for ducks.

"We'll fool those ducks," Grandpa said. "They won't be suspicious of us at all."

It was still too dark though. We had to wait until one-half hour before sunrise.

"It's important that we know the correct shooting times," Grandpa said. "Here's what we go by to know when we can shoot."

October 20

Duck Season Opens

Shooting Hours
½ hour before sunrise
to sunset

Daylight Savings Time

Date	Start	Stop
Oct. 20	6:58	6:28
Oct. 21	6:59	6:27
Oct. 22	7:00	6:25
Oct. 23	7:01	6:24
Oct. 24	7:02	6:23

Duck Season Closes

Goose Season Opens

Duck Season Opens

Shooting Hours
½ hour before sunrise
to sunset

Central Standard Time

Date	Start	Stop
Nov. 1	6:10	5:13
Nov. 2	6:12	5:12
Nov. 3	6:13	5:11
Nov. 4	6:14	5:10
Nov. 5	6:15	5:09
Nov. 6	6:16	5:08
Nov. 7	6:17	5:07
Nov. 8	6:18	5:06
Nov. 9	6:19	5:05
Nov. 10	6:20	5:04

Date	Start	Stop
Nov. 11	6:22	5:03
Nov. 12	6:23	5:02
Nov. 13	6:24	5:01
Nov. 14	6:25	5:01
Nov. 15	6:26	5:00
Nov. 16	6:27	4:59
Nov. 17	6:28	4:58
Nov. 18	6:29	4:58
Nov. 19	6:30	4:57
Nov. 20	6:32	4:56
Nov. 21	6:33	4:56
Nov. 22	6:34	4:55
Nov. 23	6:35	4:55
Nov. 24	6:36	4:54
Nov. 25	6:37	4:54
Nov. 26	6:38	4:53
Nov. 27	6:39	4:53
Nov. 28	6:40	4:53
Nov. 29	6:41	4:52
Nov. 30	6:42	4:52
Dec. 1	6:43	4:52
Dec. 2	6:44	4:52
Dec. 3	6:45	4:51
Dec. 4	6:46	4:51
Dec. 5	6:47	4:51
Dec. 6	6:48	4:51
Dec. 7	6:49	4:51
Dec. 8	6:49	4:51
Dec. 9	6:50	4:51
Dec. 10	6:51	4:51
Dec. 11	6:52	4:51
Dec. 12	6:53	4:51
Dec. 13	6:54	4:52
Dec. 14	6:54	4:52
Dec. 15	6:55	4:52

End of Duck Season

**End of
Canada Goose Season
Outside Swan Lake
Zone**

Date	Start	Stop
Dec. 16	6:56	4:52
Dec. 17	6:56	4:53
Dec. 18	6:57	4:53
Dec. 19	6:58	4:54
Dec. 20	6:58	4:54

**End of
Canada Goose Season
Inside Swan Lake
Zone**

An example of a 'shooting times' schedule.

Grandpa showed me the shooting time schedule. It gives us the time the sun comes up so that we know when we can fire our guns the first time.

Grandpa said rules and dates may be different in other states.

50

"Would you like a cup of coffee?" Grandpa offered, holding the steaming cup out to me.

"I don't drink coffee, Grandpa," I answered. "But I'd take a cup of cocoa." I knew Grandpa had a container for me. He handed me a cup and my own thermos bottle. We drank quietly and watched the sky.

"You need to button your shirt all the way to the top and stand completely still," Grandpa said. "If even that little piece of white on your T-shirt moves you'll *flare* the ducks.

"When ducks look at a pond, or any other place to land, they may see any moving object as a sign of danger," Grandpa said. "Anything out of the ordinary, especially if it moves, and the ducks will change direction and go on."

Buck, Grandpa's big Black Labrador, was excited about the hunt. He tried to sit still on the end of the boat. But we could hear him outside the gate on the blind, wiggling and whining.

"We'll have to take this guy to the draw some

51

morning," Montgomery said to Grandpa, nodding his head at me.

Montgomery didn't talk much. I hoped this would start a conversation. I had heard about the draw before. But I always loved to hear it again.

"Tell me about the draw," I said.

Grandpa and Montgomery took turns telling how all the hunters gathered at Jake's, a restaurant up the lake to the north. When the hunters got there, they would put their names in a hat. When everyone had gathered, about one and a half hours before shooting time, the first name was drawn.

That person got his choice of the fifty-eight hunting locations in Area A on Lake Odessa. The places had cool names like "The Tank", "The Northeast Slash", and "Willow Mat."

"It's a lot of *pageantry*," Grandpa said.

Then the next name was drawn and each hunter chose a spot until everyone had a place to hunt.

"It's like a game of chance," said Montgomery, "the luck of the draw. And *posturing* by the hunters. Some of them are beginning hunters who haven't learned the courtesies of duck hunting."

"You don't go there anymore, do you Grandpa?"

The ducks heard the calls. They tipped their
wings and flew toward the sound.

I had another sip of my hot cocoa. It felt good going down—nice and warm.

"Nope. Three o'clock is early enough to get up in the morning. The draw takes too much time. I like it out here in Area B where it's open. The hunting spots are not so close together."

"Look," Montgomery whispered, "here come some ducks." He looked through the binoculars. We all crouched inside the blind.

"Mallards."

Grandpa pulled his duck call to his mouth.

Squawk, squawk, quack, quack, putter, putter, putter.

Montgomery called, too. They called loudly at first. As the birds got closer, they called more quietly and less often.

The ducks heard the calls. They tipped their wings and flew toward the sound. Then they spotted the decoys and set their wings again, ready to splash into the water around the decoys.

"Get your gun up," Grandpa whispered. He and Montgomery watched the ducks closely to see what they might do. As the ducks hovered over the decoys, we all pulled our guns to our shoulders.

Bang. Bang. Bang. Two ducks fell out of the flock and splashed on the lake.

"Good shot," Grandpa said. He patted me on the back. I was pretty sure he and Montgomery had killed the ducks. Buck trembled with excitement when he heard the sound of the guns.

"Buck. Back."

Buck jumped off the front of the boat. The training with the dummies had helped Buck retrieve real ducks. He swam toward the first duck that fell. Picking it from the lake, he swam back to the boat with the green headed mallard in his mouth. I took it from him.

"Back," said Grandpa again, motioning with his arm toward where the second duck fell. Buck swam toward the second duck and brought another green head in. Again I took the duck from him. Buck loved to retrieve ducks for Grandpa.

Grandpa helped Buck get back on the end of the boat. He shook from head to toe. The icy lake water flew through the air, hitting each of us like little icicles. Buck's black coat glistened in the early morning light.

Watching Buck work was fun! He was a great water dog!

We sat down to wait for more ducks to fly over.

"Ducks land just like airplanes. Did you know that?" Grandpa asked. "They land into the wind. That's why we put the blind with its back to the wind. When the ducks fly in, they're coming right at us."

I could see why Grandpa and his friends liked duck hunting so much—ducks flying, duck calls squawking, shooting, and then watching Buck work was great fun. I hoped another flock would come in soon.

"These are drakes, the male duck," Grandpa said, holding one of the mallards Buck retrieved. "You can tell by the green head. Look at the rust-colored breast and the white stomach." Grandpa turned the mallard over in his hands. "The brown and tan speckled hens are not as pretty as the drakes."
He pulled a curly tail feather
out of the drake and handed it
to me. I tucked it into the
band around my hat.

Montgomery pulled the curly tail
feather from the other duck and added
it to the bunch of feathers on his hat brim.

"We don't shoot the hens," Grandpa said. "so there will still be mother ducks to hatch new flocks."

The duck blind was cozy and warm inside. I was glad because October mornings in Iowa can be chilly. We sat on the bench built along the center of the boat. In front of us were *LP gas* heaters for heating the blind as well as for cooking breakfast. But breakfast would not be ready until after the sun came up all the way.

We waited for a while to see if ducks were going to fly over. It was a slow morning. Grandpa and Montgomery sipped from their steaming coffee mugs. I drank some more cocoa.

"One hunt down here I had another young lad and his dad out," Grandpa said. "He was younger than you and much smaller."

Grandpa chuckled. Another of his stories was coming.

"Some ducks came in and the boy's dad said, 'Take one, Drew.' The kid was standing on the ammunition box so he could see out the hatch. He fired. The shotgun's *recoil* knocked him right off the box. We looked over at him after the flock of ducks had flown over. He was on his back in the bottom of the boat feeling pretty silly. The only thing hurt was his pride. We've chuckled about that for years."

Several wood ducks flashed by. Grandpa blew the

duck call, but they didn't come to the mallard call.

"Let's make some breakfast," Grandpa said. "How about it?"

Bacon and eggs never tasted better than when Grandpa cooked them in the big, cast-iron frying pan inside the duck blind. We ate on paper plates, balancing them on our laps.

Buck got the leftover scrambled eggs.

"Makes his coat shiny," Grandpa said.

There weren't many ducks flying. It was still early in the season. As the weather got colder, more ducks would *migrate* from the north.

"How do ducks know when to migrate south?" I asked

"It's an instinct which is created in them," Grandpa answered. "They can't think like we do and reason whether they will go south for the winter. They migrate in obedience to their instinct."

The waterfowl that fly over Lake Odessa follow traditional migratory patterns each year. They are the ducks in the Mississippi Flyway which covers the range from northern Minnesota where the Mississippi River begins all the way to where the Mississippi flows into the Gulf of Mexico.

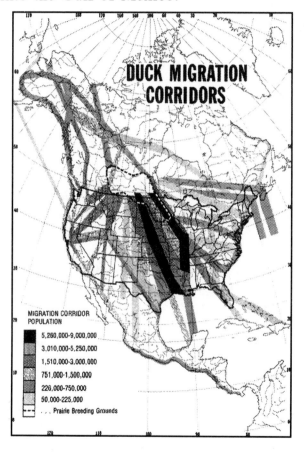

Reproduced from Ducks, Geese and Swans of North America by Frank C. Bellrose, third edition, Stackpole Books, Publishers, Third Edition. By permission of The Wildlife Management Institute.

59

DUCK CALL SOUNDS

There are many different tones and sounds that hunters can make with most any duck call:

Hail Call - loud and high pitched, the hail call gets the attention of ducks from far away.

Greeting Call - not as loud as a hail call; excited, a little faster, notes get softer as the ducks get closer to decoys.

Close-in Call - used when the ducks are swinging over the decoys; softer, contented, loafing sounds and quacks so the ducks are not frightened away.

Comeback Call - loud and demanding, trying to bring the ducks back when they have flown past the decoys.

Feeding call - a puttering sound like a duck on the water or as they fly overhead, "tic-a-tic-a-tic-a."

Lonesome hen call - soft quacks that sound like the hen mallard. Wild ducks make this sound often. Four or five notes loud, then descending to softer.

HUNTING VOCABULARY

FLARE – The ducks spread outward and change direction.

LP GAS – liquefied petroleum gas, used to operate portable stoves.

MIGRATE – to move from one place to another with the change of the seasons.

PAGEANTRY – a grand spectacle, a strange or remarkable sight.

POSTURING – a pose or an attitude just for effect.

RECOIL – the kickback that a gun does when fired.

CHAPTER SIX

WATER AND BOATING SAFETY

"Grandpa, what are some of the rules for safety in the duck blind when we're out on the water?" I asked. I wanted to be sure we were safe.

"There are many rules for water and boating safety," Grandpa answered, "and good reasons to know them. But during the duck hunting season it's especially important."

Grandpa said the two main reasons are that you go out on the water in the dark before the sun rises. And, sometimes it is dark when you come in. Hunting season is in the fall and winter when it can be cold.

"All the reasons that fit into those two are that the lake can begin to ice over very quickly if the temperature drops," Grandpa continued. "Motors are harder to start and on bigger motors the battery will operate only at partial power when it's cold. How long do you think the engine and lights will operate with a rundown battery?"

"Not long, I'll bet," I answered.

Hunting was slow.

"Montgomery, you can help us make a list," Grandpa said. He handed me a clean paper plate. He pulled a pencil out of his shirt pocket. "Write on this. Here's what you need."

Grandpa started.

"Running lights," he said. "It is a law that every boat be equipped with running lights. It is important for others who are boating on the lake or river to be able to see our light and know where we are on the water before sunrise and after sunset."

I wrote 'running lights' on the paper plate.

"The running light on the stern, which is the back of the boat, is white. It has to be up high enough to be seen by any other boat at *360 degrees*," Grandpa said.

"Three hundred sixty degrees means that someone could see it from every direction, doesn't it?"

"Yes," Grandpa answered. "And the light on the bow, or the front of the boat, is half red and half green. And it is pointed straight ahead. Are you ready to write again?"

I nodded my head and got my pencil ready.

"Life preservers. There must be a life preserver or life vest for each person on board. The life vests or preservers should be in sizes that will fit each person in the boat. If there are small people aboard, there need to be life vests to fit them.

"Not very long ago a boy and his father drowned in a river in eastern Iowa. The father didn't have a life vest, and the one the boy put on before he jumped into the river was too large for him and the river current pulled it right off of him," Montgomery said, shaking his head.

"Those were unnecessary deaths due to carelessness," Grandpa said.

I checked my life vest. It fit me. I breathed a sigh of relief. Grandpa smiled and squeezed my shoulder. He knew what I was thinking.

"If someone should fall in the lake or river there need to be throwable cushions," Montgomery said. "The kind that can be tossed to them in the water."

My list was growing. Soon I would need another plate to write on.

"An oar or paddle," Grandpa said. "Each boat must have one in case the motor doesn't run."

"What would we do if we didn't have an oar?" I asked.

"You'd be in bad shape," Grandpa said. "You'd have to depend on your horn or whistle to get some-one's attention. So add a horn or whistle to your list."

"What kind of a horn?" I asked. I pictured the squeeze horn on my bike.

"Some boats have horns built in, but you can also buy a horn with a small tank of compressed air which makes a loud blast when you squeeze it."

"What's next?"

"Have you said fire extinguisher?" Montgomery asked.

He hadn't, so I added it to my paper plate list.

"A fire extinguisher is very important," Grandpa said, "because of the cans of gasoline in the boat. The motor could catch on fire. And remember, the

"The lake can begin to ice over very quickly if the temperature drops," Grandpa said.

blind is covered with dry twigs, branches and leaves which could easily catch fire. It would be better to have an extinguisher than to have to dive into that cold lake water."

"The stove in here could start a fire, too," I added, pointing at the little cook top.

"Right!" Grandpa said. "And some people smoke cigarettes." He paused a minute and looked around the duck blind.

"You need an anchor. If the wind is blowing hard and your engine doesn't start the anchor keeps the boat from drifting so the engine can be worked on," Grandpa said. "That wouldn't be as necessary at Lake Odessa as it might be in some other body of water because there is plenty of timber that we could tie the boat up to and get it out of the wind.

"What do you think about weight, son?" Grandpa asked. "Look at all we are carrying in this boat."

Grandpa said that many hunters take too much gear in a boat that is too small and they get in trouble. They don't think about how much everything weighs.

"Our boat is licensed by the state for eight people," Grandpa said, "but with the blind, the motor, gas cans, decoys and their weights, guns and ammunition, and an eighty pound dog, there is no way we could safely carry more than four people."

"How do they decide how many people a boat can safely hold?" I asked.

"It's based on the length and size of the boat," Grandpa answered. "If the boat has a four-person load limit and the hunter takes himself and three friends and nothing else, he would probably be safe.

"I have seen boats go past that have almost no *freeboard* showing above the water," Grandpa said. "If they were on a river or a lake with large waves, one big wave and they would be *capsized*."

He pointed out that on Lake Odessa there is not much open water, so he doesn't worry about being swamped or capsized by waves.

I thought again about the boating accident Grandpa had been involved in, and that I had heard him talk about.

"Grandpa, will you tell me the story again about your boating accident in the Mississippi River?"

"It was more than twenty-five years ago now—the day before Thanksgiving Day, 1970," Grandpa said, beginning the story. "There were four of us—Bob LaFontaine, Roy Jameson, Gordon McKay, and me.

69

Two other friends had been hunting with us. They decided to stay and hunt a little longer when we left that day.

"We were in an open, 18–foot, extra–wide john boat rather than in the duck blind because of the current and the size of the Mississippi. The blind would have been too *unwieldy*.

"We had been hunting near Big Island, just below the mouth of the Skunk River south of Burlington, Iowa."

———

"We'd better call it a day and head back to the dock," Bud Hunter said. "It's getting cold."

The four men had not seen many ducks flying and decided to quit about noon on closing day of the duck hunting season.

"Brrrr," Roy Jameson said as they motored out into the river, "this wind is something fierce."

"It feels like the bottom has dropped out of the temperature," Gordon McKay said.

They were aware that the wind had picked up while they were hunting in the protected areas around the islands, but had not realized its fury on the open river.

It was blowing about thirty-five miles per hour. The strong wind meeting a strong river current head-on generated waves as high as seven feet.

"We're in trouble," Bud thought as he bailed water from around the engine. "We're taking on water," he yelled above the wind. He quickly noted that all four of them had on their life jackets.

"We're going under," Roy yelled back as the boat's bow plunged deeply into a wave and filled the boat with water. It quickly rolled over.

"Grab Gordon," Bob yelled. Gordon McKay was a giant of a man and he could not seem to hold on to the overturned boat.

"Can you talk, Gordon?"

There was no answer. Only a gurgling sound came from his throat. He drifted off the boat. Quietly and diligently the men took turns trying to hoist their friend back onto the overturned boat.

"We'll have to let him go," Roy said. "He's gone. We need to preserve our strength to stay alive."

The men began to yell for help, waiting after each yell, hoping beyond hope that someone out there would hear them.

Barge traffic had stopped for the year. No boats

71

were on the river.

"You doin' okay?" Roy asked, questioning both Bob and Bud. He called on all the survival training he had used as an Air Force pilot. "We've got to hold on!" he said emphatically. "Stay with the boat!"

The cold water began to take its toll on all three of the men. *Hypothermia* lulled them into a false sense of well being. Their words to each other became fewer. All they could do was yell.

"Help!"

Meanwhile, the two men in the other boat were still hunting back by Big Island. Mel DeLang shot a duck. It landed on shore.

"Let's go get that duck," Mel said, "then we'd better call it a day, too."

They motored over to the shore and beached their john boat. Howie Holzen, driving the boat shut off the engine.

"I can hear some geese," he said. "Listen."

Mel turned his face into the wind to listen.

"Those aren't geese," Mel answered. "That's somebody hollering for help."

They jumped back into their boat and, as fast as the current and the waves permitted, they motored toward the middle of the river. They spotted someone waving. The men hung on to the overturned boat.

"They're in trouble," Mel shouted. He calculated how long ago they had left the hunting party. "They've been in the water a long time—near an hour."

"Help!" the three remaining voices called from the river.

Both Mel and Howie began to try and lift the wet hunters aboard their boat realizing that five soaked men could endanger their boat, too.

"Grab Hunter," Roy said.

Mel reached for the suspenders on Bud's waders. The suspenders broke and he went completely under. Mel grabbed again when he surfaced and got him into the boat.

With their boat completely full they carefully began to head south with the river and toward the bank.

"Come on, Bud, get your face out of the water," Roy said, as he turned his friend's head out of the water in the bottom of the boat to keep him from drowning. Bud was so far gone that he couldn't even raise himself up.

"What happened to Gordon?" Mel asked.

"We think he had a heart attack when he hit the cold water," Roy said. "We finally had to let him go and he floated away."

Mel and Howie, both sitting in the back of the boat to keep the bow up out of the water, nosed the boat against the shore of an island and pulled all the men to safety.

"Bring me the gas can," Mel ordered. Howie rushed to get it and helped Mel douse an abandoned duck blind to set it on fire.

"Strip off your clothes," Mel said to the wet men. He helped them get out of their waders and their wet clothing.

They all hunkered around the roaring fire and began to thaw out.

Mel and Howie both took off all their outer clothing and divided it among the other three men. Dressed only in a T-shirt and his waders Howie left the island to go for help. Mel, similarly dressed, stayed with the recovering men.

I got up and paced a few steps in the duck blind. Montgomery had been quiet as he listened again to the tale of his friend's rescue.

"I hate that story, Grandpa," I said. "Just think, I might never have known you. But I love the story because you are alive! What happened next?"

Grandpa stood. He hitched up his chest waders.

"I'm glad to be alive, too," he said. "All of us were taken to the hospital in Burlington where they treated us for exposure and let us go home. The authorities were called and they began to look for Gordon's body. They found him very quickly."

"Did you think you would never duck hunt again, Grandpa?"

"Oh, no. I was sure that I'd hunt again," Grandpa said. "But I would never again be excited about going on the Mississippi River in November. And I still miss my old friend, Gordon."

We had already talked about clothing but Grandpa said again how important warm clothing is during cold and unpredictable weather.

"Too many clothes is far better than too few," he said.

"What if something happened on Lake Odessa and we couldn't get back to the shore? What would we do?" I asked.

"I always try to tell someone where I'm going and about what time they can expect me back," Grandpa said, "so that they will know where to look for me if I don't show up."

"What could we do to help ourselves?" I thought about the miracle of Mel and Howie turning off their boat engine and hearing my grandpa and his friends calling for help.

"If the engine wouldn't start, we could use our paddle and get the boat or duck blind out into a part of the lake where other boats are," Grandpa said. He thought some more. "On Lake Odessa you could paddle up against the land and walk until you came to a cabin.

"One thing for sure, you shouldn't wait until the last minute to quit hunting if your equipment has not been working properly," Grandpa said.

"Usually it doesn't quit working from one minute to the next," Montgomery said. "The problem has been coming on for a while.

"If it gets dark, you can shine your light or shoot

your gun," Grandpa said. "If someone is out there and their motor isn't running they might hear you."

My grandfather has some hair-raising stories to tell about experiences on the lake. He has learned many things about the changeability of the weather, and the necessity for boating safety.

I'm going to a boating safety course to learn more about boats and water safety.

VOCABULARY WORDS

360 DEGREES – one complete turn around a circle.

CAPSIZED – to overturn or upset, or sink a boat.

FREEBOARD – the distance from the main deck to the waterline of a ship. In small boats, it is the amount of boat that is visible above the water.

HYPOTHERMIA – subnormal body temperature.

UNWIELDY – hard to handle because of large size or weight.

CHAPTER SEVEN

PUDDLE DUCKS

"Many people think that duck hunting means hunting only mallards," Grandpa said. "Do you know how many species of puddle ducks there are?"

"I know about wood ducks and teal—the blue-winged and the green-winged," I answered. "Are there many more?"

"Remember the duck hanging by the fireplace at my house?" Grandpa asked.

"The black duck? Is that a puddle duck?"

"It sure is," Grandpa said. "In fact the hen's call is similar to a mallard's. Then there are pintails, widgeons, gadwalls, and shovelers."

The ducks that we hunted at Lake Odessa were puddle ducks. Puddle ducks liked water that wasn't deep—like marshes and ponds, the backwaters of large rivers, and small lakes, and the bays of larger lakes.

They came to feed on the *submerged* plant life.

"The state wildlife *biologists* sometimes sow *millet* in the lake," Grandpa said. "Millet is a cereal grain that grows in the water for the ducks to feed on. But ducks sometimes also feed early in the morning on wasted grain in farm fields.

"If they're eating in the fields, sometimes around mid–morning they might return to the lake or back-water where they spend the night. Sometimes they'll fly out again in the mid–afternoon and come back to the water at sunset."

Grandpa said ducks are unpredictable. They feed sometimes on a moonlit night, and often feed any time of day, especially if a storm was coming.

"Are there more mallards than any other kind of puddle duck, Grandpa?" I asked.

"Yes, they are the most plentiful of the puddle ducks," Grandpa confirmed. "You can identify them by the violet–blue *speculum*, a distinctive patch of color on the wing, which you can see when they sit on the water. You've already seen how flashy their heads are—a beautiful *iridescent* green color."

Mallards are the most plentiful puddle ducks.

"Sometimes when we hunt you try to call to a flock of wood ducks," I said, "but they don't come to the mallard call. What kind of call do wood ducks make?"

"Theirs is a squeaking noise," Grandpa said. "Woodies may not be as plentiful as mallards, but they are America's prettiest ducks. You can watch for their blue and purple top-knot of feathers and the gold under their wings."

Grandpa explained that wood ducks were once almost *extinct*. Now they are the second most-harvested duck in Iowa.

"Years ago the federal government closed the hunting season on woodies," Grandpa said. "There would be no shooting."

Sportsmen built wood duck houses and hung them in the timber on the islands around and in the lake. This improved the birds nesting *habitat* and proved to be a big help. Boy Scouts and conservation clubs built and erected nesting boxes in most every state and assisted in the wood duck's return to plentiful numbers.

"Woodies are in good supply again. Thanks to the conservationists, they've made an amazing recovery." Montgomery explained.

"Hunters are allowed to take a limit of two wood ducks during the regular Iowa duck hunting season," Grandpa said. "The limits are subject to change and you always need to know the laws for each hunting season."

"I wonder how long it will take before I can recognize which kind of duck is flying over? How did you guys ever learn to know which duck is which?" I asked.

"It just takes time studying them and memorizing their features," Grandpa answered. "Their body size and wing beat are clues when they are flying toward us. You watch the next flock of Canada geese and see how slow their wings beat compared to a flock of mallards.

"Watch how the ducks circle the pond or landing site," Grandpa said. "They will sometimes fly around several times checking it over to see if there is danger. If they don't see anything, then they plop into the water. Puddle ducks all have larger wings which give them the ability to *maneuver*."

Grandpa pointed out that puddle ducks ride higher in the water than diving ducks. Their tails show above the water line.

About mid–morning we gave up and headed for the dock. The weather forecast was for the temperature to drop and the wind to change direction and come in from the north/northwest.

"That should bring more new ducks in," Grandpa said. "We'll go back out mid–afternoon to hunt again before sunset."

I felt like I had been in school. I had learned so much about hunting.

HUNTING VOCABULARY

BIOLOGIST – a person who deals with plant and animal life.

EXTINCT – no longer in existence.

HABITAT – the area in which birds and animals live; their natural environment.

IRIDESCENT – showing a shifting interplay of rainbow-like colors.

MANEUVER – a skillful change in movement or direction.

MILLET – a cereal grass whose small grain is used to feed the wildfowl.

SPECULUM – a patch of color on the wings of certain birds, especially ducks.

SUBMERGED – covered with water.

OTHER PUDDLE DUCKS

WOOD DUCKS

Wood ducks can be identified in flight by their long, squared-off tails. The drake is distinctive and beautiful. The hen is more plain. Both the drake and the hen have a crested head—the drake's an iridescent purple-green-crest, with white throat and cheek patches. The hen has a distinctive teardrop-shaped eye ring on her gray head. The red eyes and red at the base of its bill clearly identifies the wood duck.

BLACK DUCK

The black duck is sometimes called a black mallard, but their speculum does not have the violet-blue markings of the mallard. The body of both the drake and hen is brownish-black.

PINTAIL

Pintail ducks are named for the drake's long, pointed tail. They have a chocolate brown head with a white line extending up the long neck. The wings are longer and narrower than those of other ducks.

TEAL

The teal are the smallest of the puddle ducks with blue-winged teals weighing about one pound and green-winged teals about three-fourths of a pound. Teal are acrobatic ducks, darting, twisting and turning like shorebirds in flight. The blue-winged teal drake has a gray blue patch on the leading edge of their wings and a white crescent in front of their eyes. The green-winged teal drake has a chestnut brown head with a dark green ear patch.

AMERICAN WIDGEON

The widgeon is sometimes called a baldpate because of the drake's white crown, making it look bald-headed. A dark green band extends from its eyes to the back of its head. Females are the same brownish- gray of most hens except their sides are rust colored.

GADWALL

Also called the "gray duck," gadwalls resemble widgeons, but they lack the white patch on the leading edge of the wings and the white crown on the drake's head.

CHAPTER EIGHT

CLEANING THE DUCKS

"I sure could use a nap," Montgomery said. He left the idea hanging in the air.

"We'd better clean these ducks first," Grandpa said. Then when he considered that we only had three ducks to clean he said, "You go ahead and start your nap. My hunting buddy and I will clean them."

He looked at me and smiled. He handed one of the ducks to me.

I really didn't like this part of duck hunting.

"You'll get used to it," Grandpa said. "It won't bother you after you clean a few."

"Back a few years ago," Grandpa started to say. He pulled feathers off one of the ducks we had shot this morning. A comfortable silence hung between us.

Grandpa pulled the feathers off of a duck
we had shot.

"What happened, Grandpa?" I prompted him to go ahead and tell his story. I watched as he began to clean the duck. I tried to do the same motions with the duck I was cleaning. I wasn't as fast as Grandpa.

"We used to shoot so many ducks that we had someone else clean them. There were many more ducks back then. So we took them to Pearly Mae for cleaning."

This sounded like another one of Grandpa's interesting folk tales.

"Who was Pearly?"

"Pearly and her sister lived in Wapello in a little old house in the south end of town. They earned their living in those days by cleaning ducks and geese for the many men who hunted in and around Lake Odessa. They were known for miles around," Grandpa said.

Montgomery hadn't gone in for his nap yet. He was sitting on the bottom step of the porch.

"Remember them, Montgomery?"

"I sure do. We'd carry

90

our ducks to Wapello after our hunt and take them to Pearly's house," Montgomery said. "Her kitchen would be full of ducks. Every pot and pan, the double sink, and sometimes newspapers on the floor would be covered with ducks."

Grandpa laughed heartily.

"One time we stopped at Pearly's at noon time. She and her sister were eating their lunch. Right in the middle of all those ducks!" Grandpa laughed again. "Both of them had on big aprons that covered their whole front. Those aprons were **covered** with duck feathers. They looked more like ducks than the ducks."

We all laughed.

"I sure couldn't eat lunch right now," I said looking at the yukky mess of blood and feathers. "Not with this mess. Could you Grandpa?"

He and Montgomery both agreed that they wouldn't want to eat with all the duck feathers around.

"Pearly and her sister are both gone now," Grandpa said, "and we don't shoot enough ducks anymore that anyone could earn a living at cleaning them. So we have to clean them ourselves."

We kept pulling feathers.

"Ducks are harder to clean when they get cold," Grandpa said. "We probably should pick them while we're still in the blind—while their bodies are warm. Then the feathers come off real easy."

"Those look like young ducks," Montgomery added. "Their pin feathers are harder to get off."

Grandpa had me use the pliers to pull them out.

 "When we get down to the little, downy feathers, there's another way to get them off, but it's kind of a mess, too," Grandpa said. "I've melted *paraffin* in boiling water and dipped the bird in it. When the paraffin hardens, you can pull it off. The feathers are supposed to come with it. Most often it works.

"Your grandmother and I don't eat wild ducks any—more. Grandma doesn't like to cook them," Grandpa said.

So Grandpa cleaned and wrapped all his ducks and gave them away. There were several men who had been great hunters but they couldn't go in the duck blinds because of their health.

They were pleased when Grandpa brought them wild game along with some wild rice from Minnesota.

My grandpa knows a lot about duck hunting. I have learned so much about hunting from him. I hope you've learned something from reading about our hunts.

If you have an interest in hunting, fishing, the outdoors, or conservation, maybe your grandfather, dad or an uncle can help you learn more. If not, your public library or a book store would be a good place to start.

Your state's conservation commission sponsors 'hunter safety courses.' These are taught by local sportsmen. The classes often are taught over a weekend. The local newspaper would be a place to check for dates for the next course.

If the newspaper can't help you, many local clubs such as the Izaak Walton League, Ducks Unlimited, the Wildlife Federation or a trap shooting range can help with your education and pleasure.

Ducks Unlimited has a special 'Green Wing' membership and magazine for young folks under the age of sixteen.

HUNTING VOCABULARY

PARAFFIN – a white, waxy, odorless and tasteless substance from which candles are made. Also used to seal canning jars and for waterproofing paper.

A HUNTER'S PLEDGE

Responsible hunting provides unique challenges and rewards. However, the future of the sport depends on each hunter's behavior and ethics. Therefore, as a hunter, I pledge to:

- Respect the environment and wildlife.
- Respect property and landowners.
- Show consideration for nonhunters.
- Hunt safely.
- Know and obey the law.
- Pass on an ethical hunting tradition.
- Strive to improve my outdoor skills and understanding of wildlife.
- Hunt only with ethical hunters.

By following these principles of conduct each time I go afield, I will give my best to the sport, the public, the environment and myself. The responsibility to hunt ethically is mind; the future of hunting depends on me.

_____

My Name

This pledge was created by a number of hunting and conservation organizations and funders interested in promoting hunting ethics.

For more information, write the Izaak Walton League of America, 1401 Wilson Blvd., Level B; Arlington, VA 22209-2318.

ENDNOTES

'Grandpa' in this story is C.F. 'Bud' Hunter, well-known Iowa sportsman and fisherman. Bud has taught many young men to shoot and call ducks, and has been their guide and teacher through many successful duck hunts in the 'bottoms' of Lake Odessa, which is the location of a federal wildlife refuge in southeastern Iowa.

Bud's old cabin on Lake Odessa has been a resting place of hunters from across the nation as they have come to be guided in a duck hunt by the respected outdoorsman. Hearing their praise for the good time, the good food, and the good hunt, one would think they had stayed at a swanky hotel.

Bud was chosen the Iowa State Duck Calling Champion in Des Moines, Iowa in 1969, after having been first runner-up the previous year. He taught duck calling at Kirkwood Community College in Cedar Rapids, Iowa, and for a short time manufactured 'Bud Hunter Duckcalls.'

Bud has been the owner of a number of quality Labrador Retrievers. He has worked actively as a member of Ducks Unlimited (DU) for the past thirty years to make the local chapter a successful group in providing funds for wildlife habitat. He is a National Trustee Emeritus of Ducks Unlimited.

The Cedar Rapids Chapter of DU honored him one year at their annual sponsor dinner as the member having contributed more to young people's hunting skills than any other member.

Bud is a semi-retired real estate appraiser. He enjoys hunting, fishing, and playing golf. He looks forward to spending many years in the duck blind with his sons, sons-in-law, grandsons, granddaughters, and friends.

THE BOY IN THE STORY

The character from whose point-of-view this story is written is fictional but he could be any one of several boys including Bud's sons, Kevin and John, or his grandsons, Sam, Jacob, or Joshua. Perhaps he's a composite of them all.

ABOUT THE AUTHOR

Helen Hunter is 'Grandpa's' wife. She, too, is a wildlife enthusiast and supports her husband's hunting hobby and participates in his fishing hobby.

Helen is president of Hunter & Associates, book-sellers to public libraries across the nation.

She has had numerous articles and stories for children and adults published in a wide variety of magazines and journals, and one non-fiction book for adults. This is her first book for children.

Besides writing and bookselling, Helen is a full time college student.

She loves spending time with her children and grandchildren in addition to participating in vocal music, and in Bible study and church activities.

ABOUT THE ILLUSTRATOR

Grant Rozeboom, from Middle Amana, Iowa, drew the pencil sketches for this book when he was ten years old. The cover, done in oil, was completed at the age of twelve.

When Grant was ten years old, his acrylic painting of a lone blue goose was awarded Best of Show in the Iowa State Junior Duck Stamp Competition. It went on to win top-ten honors in the National Junior Duck Stamp design contest.

His parents, Lori and Glenn Rozeboom, home-schooled Grant for his elementary years. During those years he studied art with his grandfather, Jack Hahn, nationally recognized decoy carver and wildlife painter from the Amana Colonies. Since Jack Hahn went home to be with the Lord in February 1997, Grant studies art with artist Charles Freitag from Reinbeck, Iowa. He is currently attending a private Christian school.

Besides art, Grant also enjoys and is very active in soccer, basketball, church youth group, and music.

TO ORDER ADDITIONAL COPIES OF THIS BOOK

Phone (319) 362-4777

or write

Hunter & Associates
1132 21st Street S.E.
Cedar Rapids, IA 52403

Enclose $8.40 (includes Iowa Sales Tax)
plus $1.50 shipping and handling

Make check or money order payable to:

Hunter & Associates

Please allow 3-4 weeks for delivery

You may write the author at:

1132 21st Street S.E.
Cedar Rapids, IA 52403

You may write the illustrator at:

P. O. Box 151
Middle Amana, IA 52307–0151

Printed in the USA by

MORRIS PUBLISHING

3212 East Highway 30 • Kearney, NE 68847 • 1-800-650-7888